Praise for 7

"Ashley-Smith debuts with a gorgeous, melancholy coming-of-age novella about girlhood and ghosts. ... This eerie, ethereal tale marks Ashley-Smith as a writer to watch."
—Publishers Weekly

"A beautifully written book about desire, pain, and loss, haunted by glimmerings of the supernatural. *The Attic Tragedy* manages to do more by intimation and suggestion with its fifty-three pages than most novels manage to accomplish over their several hundred."
—Brian Evenson, author of *Song for the Unraveling of the World*

"J. Ashley-Smith doesn't put a foot wrong in this chilling, devastating story. *The Attic Tragedy* is hard to read in the best possible way."
—Kaaron Warren, award-winning author of
Into Bones Like Oil and *Tide of Stone*

"J. Ashley-Smith's stunning *The Attic Tragedy* follows the friendship between two young outcasts, Sylvie and George, as they navigate the treacherous years of high school and after. With piercing, clear-eyed sympathy, Ashley-Smith depicts a relationship centered on the secrets of the living and the dead. Sylvie knows and voices the histories of the spirits attached to the objects in her father's antique shop; George wrestles with the emotions raging within her and which find their outlet on her skin. Acutely observed, frequently surprising, this is fiction of the highest order."
—John Langan, author of
Children of the Fang and Other Genealogies

"Lyrical and melancholy, *The Attic Tragedy* is a dark and poignant study of what it means to love and to be loved, to lose and to be lost. Ashley-Smith conjures a compelling, haunting tale that will stay with you like a ghost long after the last page is read."
—Alan Baxter, award-winning author of
Devouring Dark and *Served Cold*

"*The Attic Tragedy* is full of heart and darkness, both endearing and terrifying. These pages open like a raw wound. You don't read this story. It bleeds into you, and it leaves a scar on the way in."
—Sarah Read, Bram Stoker Award® winning author of
The Bone Weaver's Orchard and *Out of Water*

"*The Attic Tragedy* is beautifully engrossing, elegant, and lavish in the traditions of ornate architecture: J. Ashley-Smith's exquisite words are its sculpted stone blocks; his layers of resonant emotions their subtle coloring treatments; his backdrop of ghosts those detailed flourishes that drive all expressive design to be admired for impression and refinement."
—Eric J. Guignard, award-winning author and editor, including
That Which Grows Wild and *Doorways to the Deadeye*

"Softly shrouded in smoke and shadow, Ashley-Smith's *The Attic Tragedy* cuts close to the bone. Startling, pointed, and powerful."
—Lee Murray, three-time Bram Stoker Award®
nominee and author of *Into the Ashes*

"With *The Attic Tragedy*, J. Ashley-Smith proves himself an elemental writer of great talent. Emotions are bushfires. Foggy mountains shadow streets where violence festers. Dust, the microbes of otherness, settle over empty rooms that are never as empty as you think they are. This attic is a place of patchwork-detail where characters are forced to question their legacies, and I was held captive by their frightening revelations. A moody, melancholic read that I can't recommend highly enough."

—Aaron Dries, author of *House of Sighs* and *A Place for Sinners*

"J. Ashley-Smith's short novella, *The Attic Tragedy*, is a sharp and delicate jewel that both shines beautifully and cuts deeply. Focusing on the friendship of two girls, it slowly unveils a deep sense of strangeness and dread, both puzzling and fascinating. Masterly crafted, it will please all lovers of Shirley Jackson, who will be thrilled to find again this mix of humanity, beauty and cruelty."

—Seb Doubinsky, author of *Missing Signal* and *The Invisible*

"A tale of loss, trauma and identity, masterfully told. Horror and thriller elements underpin an unsettling coming-of-age story . . . Ashley-Smith's style is gripping, his structure clear and considered. *The Attic Tragedy*'s multifaceted nature and effective storytelling has far-reaching appeal."

—Aurealis Magazine

THE ATTIC TRAGEDY

a novelette by

J. ASHLEY-SMITH

Meerkat Press
Atlanta

One line from The Oresteia by Aeschylus, translated by Robert Fagles
Copyright © Robert Fagles 1966, 1967, 1975, 1977

ISBN-13: 978-1-946154-48-4 (Paperback)
ISBN-13 978-1-946154-49-1 (eBook)

Library of Congress Control Number: 2020938666

Book cover and interior design by Tricia Reeks

Printed in the United States of America

Published in the United States of America by
Meerkat Press, LLC, Atlanta, Georgia
www.meerkatpress.com

To K, for the enduring love of stories locked in strange
old things.

Dear gods, set me free from all the pain.
—Aeschylus

Prologos

Sylvie never called them ghosts, but that's what they were.

The day we became friends, she walked me through the darkened rooms of her father's antique shop, trailing her fingers over the objects. All of them were lovingly cleaned, none with even a trace of dust. There were old books and reliquaries, trinket jars and model ships, barometers, credenzas, compendiums and lamps. There were music boxes and what I now know was a Minton hand-painted jardinière. Sylvie brushed them with her long pale fingers, her eyes aflutter, her voice so soft it was almost lost to the tinkle of the overhead chandeliers, the *tick tick tick* of the many hidden clocks.

"The woman who wore this lost her husband to madness." Sylvie fingered an ornate ring, curlicued silver bordered with diamonds. "He disappeared when she fell pregnant and everyone thought him dead. He'd been gone three years when she read about him in the paper. He was living rough in Centennial Park, running naked and wild, biting the heads off geese." She slipped the ring back into its padded velvet tray. "Her mother always said he'd come to no good."

"Or this," she said, and her fingers moved to the stem of a burnished brass telescope. "A lover's memento. The woman who owned this took a keepsake from every man she fell for. Not one of them ever knew of her love. And none loved her in return. She died of loneliness and an overdose of laudanum, lifted from the Gladstone of a doctor she'd set her heart on."

Sylvie swam between display cases with fluid movements, her touch as delicate as a butterfly. I hardly dared move, afraid my bulk would knock over some priceless curio, topple some fragile ancient thing.

"How do you know?" I asked and followed, squeezing between a bookcase and a mahogany sideboard. A blue glass vase wobbled on its shelf and I reached out to steady it. "D'you find all that on the Internet or something?"

"No, silly," said Sylvie, eyes laughing. "They *tell* me."

I thought she was teasing, so turned away, pretended I was examining the collectables. Beside us was a heavy leather-top desk, the surface inlaid with gold leaf that glittered faintly in the half-light. There was an old-fashioned cash register and a marble bust and, beside them, a black-and-white photo in a silver art deco frame. It was a portrait of a dark-haired woman with round faraway eyes and a haunting smile; just as Sylvie would look in ten years, twenty years—beautiful and tired and sad. But there was a spark in her eyes, as though she were smiling through the sadness, like a single beam of sunlight glimpsed through brooding clouds.

"And this one?" I said and reached to pick it up, but felt through my sweater a delicate touch. Sylvie's hand on my arm.

I felt hot all over and prayed I wasn't blushing. Every one of my scars was tingling. "What do you mean they tell you? Like you can . . . *hear* them?"

Sylvie looked up at me and frowned, her eyebrows furrowed and serious.

"Of course," she said. "You mean you *can't?*"

Parados

Sylvie joined our school in the year before final exams. Graceful and etheric, dressed in a pale, simple frock, white cotton gloves and clutching an old-fashioned leather satchel, she looked like a creature from another time. She was quiet in class, didn't play sport, kept herself to herself.

She was hardly the first out-of-place teenager at Blackworth High School. There'd always been a steady turnover of tree-changer offspring, dragged to the mountains by parents fleeing the bustle of city life. These kids knew they were different from us, knew they stood out. They went out of their way to ingratiate themselves—coarsened their accents, roughened their polished city edges, fell too quickly in line with the will of the schoolyard leaders. But not Sylvie. She made no effort to connect, spoke always in the same soft, cultivated tone, was forever daydreaming, always preoccupied. Her lack of deference did not go unnoticed.

Tansy Rimer and her gang of pretties sniffed around for a week or two but gave up in disgust, told everyone Sylvie was a stuck-up bitch with tickets on herself. The quiet boys watched and pined, too afraid to approach the sweet new girl with her distant warmth and faraway eyes. Tommy Payne and his thugs jostled and joshed whenever she passed, made mucky remarks and filthy gestures, their laughter echoing down the corridors.

I saw her, sometimes, beneath the stands of conifer trees, drifting along the edge of the oval, while the other kids pushed and yelled, playing soccer or basketball. Sylvie had a note that kept her off all games, inside and outside, and this escape—from what to most was school's central purpose and to the rest was its central humiliation—only served to alienate her further.

I didn't go in for sport much either, spending break and afternoon games in the library. There's only so many times you can endure the indignity of being picked last, the look of revulsion on Tansy's face or the faces of her lieutenant bitches, the nauseated groans when they lost the lottery and had to have me on their team. They used to yell at me as I lumbered around the field, tripped me if I ever came near the ball. They sang "Georgie Porgie" and changed the words, tried to make me cry.

The library was my escape. I didn't read all that much, but I liked to handle the books, liked the smell of them, the quiet. Miss Terry, the librarian, was always kind to me, always called me George. Never my hated name. I helped her with the catalog, stuck new labels on the inside pages, wheeled the trolley of returns up and down the fluorescent-lit aisles. I liked sorting the books into piles, into subjects, into alphabetical order, then slipping them back onto the shelves, always in just the right spot. Each one of them had a home, a place where it and no other belonged. It gave me a good feeling to know that, in at least this one corner of the world, I brought some semblance of order to what would otherwise be chaos. Here, at least, there was something I could control.

I watched Sylvie from the library window, watched her float round the edges of the courtyard. Perhaps I saw something in her that reminded me of myself; on the surface we couldn't have been more unalike, but in our isolation, in our status as outsiders, we were very much the same. I'd watch her drift out beyond the thresholds of the playing field, as though pulled by some invisible thread, guided by inaudible voices.

~

At the farthest corner of the oval, out where the monkey puzzle trees met the train tracks, there was a derelict maintenance shed. It had been abandoned since the school got its extension and was all but empty, with the only reminders to its intended purpose rolls of chain-link fence and a heap of star pickets. It was hidden from most of the school buildings, tucked round to the side. The only place you could see it from inside was the window in the library storeroom.

Everyone knew Tommy took girls back there to do things. More than once I'd been loading the trolley with returns, had seen from the window one or another Year Ten girl come out from behind that old shed with her hair in a tangle, tugging at her undies or wiping at her skirt. Sometimes there were tears. Always there'd be a plume of bluish smoke that rose from behind the shed, before Tommy Payne—sometimes Darren and Boz too—would come swaggering out and back to school.

I never understood why they went there, those girls, whether stripping naked for Tommy in the lee of that old shed was a choice they made themselves, or one that was made for them. No matter how much of a shit we all knew Tommy to be, he never wanted for admirers. There was always some half-broken waif from the year below who'd fall into a trance when Tommy strode down the corridor. Often it was those same girls coming out from behind the shed, making that walk of shame. Sometimes there were photos. The boys would load them to the Internet, or everybody's phones would beep and there'd be sniggers and jeers. One time, after, a girl killed herself and we—all of us—pretended not to know the reason.

It made me boil to think of it, what Tommy and his boys got

away with, knowing what was happening and having no power to do anything. I often pictured it—wheeling the trolley from aisle to aisle, or making space on the shelves for the new editions—pictured what I'd do to them. But that only made me boil all the more, made my scars sing, knowing pictures were all they'd ever be and that nobody would make those boys stop. Me, least of all.

~

It was November when it happened, the first hot days after a long, cold spring. For weeks before, the mountain had been pressed under a blanket of fog and drizzle, breaking only to erupt into storms of wild rain, black clouds that roiled and tumbled in from the valley and thunder that shook every weatherboard along the ridge. That morning, though, the rain cleared and by first break the sun had burned away the last of the milky fog. By lunch, it was like the past weeks had never been. There was no moisture in the air; the heat was oppressive. Just walking between classes had me sweating so bad that my school shirt was sodden and I had to pull on my morning sweater to cover the stains spreading around my armpits. The heat was unbearable beneath that scratchy wool, but better to be hot than seen. It was an enormous relief to get into the library, out of the sunlight, away from the taunts, to be slowly cooled by occasional gusts from the air conditioner.

I pushed the book trolley over to my favorite spot by the window. From there I could shuffle the books around, lay them out in order before wheeling them to their stacks. I could keep one eye on the world outside, maybe catch a glimpse of Sylvie. I'd got used to seeing her pass beneath the covered walkway outside the library windows, past the Principal's office and the portable classrooms, out to the edge of the oval and the chain-link fence and the train tracks beyond. I'd come to look forward to the moment when she'd drift past, buoyant, as though afloat in some sublime ether only she could perceive. Those moments for me felt eternal, frozen in time. The light was perfect as a dream. My heart would blaze and my scars sing, and my true body would tingle and vibrate with an aliveness so intense it made me dizzy, made me almost believe I could burst free from this prison of flesh.

That day, when Sylvie passed, I pretended to be engrossed in the trolley, in slipping the unread copy of *Ulysses* in beside the dog-eared *Nancy Drews*. When I looked up, there she was, crossing the oval, her head in the clouds. She was so lost in herself that she didn't notice Tommy Payne and his boys sneaking behind her, following her out to the edge of the grounds, out toward the derelict maintenance shed.

Then they passed beyond the corner of the school and I lost sight of them.

I stuffed the books I'd been sorting onto the shelves at random, pushed the still-full trolley out to the back of the library, into the storeroom and over to the window. There was the shed, and there was Sylvie, drifting, oblivious. Tommy Payne was closing the gap, Darren and Boz behind, clowning, making dirty gestures, laughing silently. I lurched away from the trolley, caught it with my thigh as I turned and the books went flying, James Joyce and Carolyn Keene and all the rest of them.

"George?" said Miss Terry. But I didn't answer, didn't have the breath.

Out of the doors, across the courtyard and onto the oval. I couldn't see Sylvie or Tommy or any of them anywhere. I felt sick to my guts, suddenly desperate for the loo. I lumbered over the grass, a stitch burning in my chest, sweat pouring off me so thick it was in my eyes, my ears. I heard voices from behind the shed, cruel laughter, and jeering. As I passed the heaps of coiled fencing, I snatched up a star picket, hefting it like a club. With no idea what I was doing or why I was doing it, I stepped round the side of the shed to face them.

"Leave her alone," I said, trying to make my voice as deep and threatening as a boy's.

"Fuck me," said Tommy. "It's the Hulk."

Darren and Boz turned and both of them laughed. Tommy had Sylvie against the wall of the shed, gripping her bare arm. She recoiled from the touch, her face crumpled. I saw she was missing a glove.

"I said leave her alone." I took a step toward them, tried to lift the picket but I was so scared my arms were like jelly.

Tommy sneered. "Or what, lezzer? You'll drown us in blubber?"

"Yeah," said Darren and they laughed again. "Fuck off, ya fat cunt."

Maybe it was that word, or their sneering grins, or the helpless look on Sylvie's face, but something in me flashed, as fierce and frenzied as a bushfire. I roared and swung the picket at Tommy. It was heavier than I thought and my aim was off, so I missed him by a mile. The picket struck the hard ground, bounced up and into Boz's shin. He buckled, yelled. Tommy lowered his brows, growled, dropped Sylvie's arm. He stepped away from the shed, fists clenched like hammers.

"You try that again," said Tommy, stepping toward me. "You just try that again, you rug-munching bitch."

Darren was coming at me from the left, Tommy from the front. I dragged the picket up in a ponderous arc, slammed the sharp end into Tommy's privates. He dropped, howling. Darren grabbed me from behind and I arched, felt his nose crack off the back of my head. I whirled, spun the picket up and out, felt the vibration all the way up my arms as it struck the side of Boz's head like a bell. He pitched forward, blood bursting from his ear. I lifted the picket and smacked it down on Tommy, still rolling at my feet, cupping his balls. I raised it again and would've slammed it down again, would've smashed it and kept on smashing, turned that rotten bugger's skull into watermelon—if it weren't for Sylvie. I felt a soft tugging at my sleeve and she was beside me.

"Come on," she said. "We need to go."

I dropped the picket and stumbled after her—away from the boys groaning in the dirt behind the shed, hands pressed to noses, ears and nuts—followed her back toward the school and our afternoon class.

⁓

That night, after helping Mum into bed and turning out the lights all through the house, I locked myself in the bathroom, popped the lid on the old tobacco tin and laid out all my treasures along the edge of the bath. They glinted sweetly and my scars sang. But I didn't pick one. I just sat there on the edge of the loo, my clothes heaped by the bathroom door.

After a time, I picked up the tin, put back the treasures one by one. I tucked the tin away in the space beneath the bath, replaced the loose tile to cover it, tossed my clothes in the laundry bin and went back to my bedroom.

I dreamed of fences and an empty house beyond the train tracks.

⁓

It wasn't the perfect way to start a friendship, but it did bring us together. I walked Sylvie home after school that day, back to the antique shop; that was when she showed me the ring and the telescope, told me all those strange things.

I'd felt sick to my guts all afternoon, couldn't focus on a word in double history. I kept waiting for the door to fly open, for the Principal to come in and stop the class, beckon me with a finger. Tommy's chair was empty. Neither he nor Darren nor Boz showed up for the rest of that day. Nor the day after that. The worry that I had done them serious damage grew into anxiety that they were lying in wait, planning retribution.

In the days and weeks to come, that feeling stretched as fine and taut as my nerves. I never told anyone about it. Only Sylvie knew what really happened that day. The boys never told either, too embarrassed maybe that it was me that did them over. When they came back to school, they laughed it off, said they'd got into a fight in town. But in class, I felt the tingle of Tommy's eyes boring into me. Walking to and from school, either alone, or with Sylvie on the way up the High Street toward her father's shop, I'd cast glances over my shoulder, jerk my head at any unexpected movement. But I never did catch sight of Tommy or his boys.

Friendship with Sylvie was like a balm that settled the churning in my belly, soothed my agitation; her small, unbidden gestures of tenderness, her sweet and powdery scent. I was a stranger to intimacy and this new closeness ignited a flame that flickered deep within my ribcage, a true-body flame that warmed me even through all those layers of meat and bone.

～

One Saturday, toward the end of term, I met Sylvie at the edge of town and we took a path through the woods to the reservoir. At the eastern end, there was a car park and a playground with barbecues and picnic tables. At the other, a wood crisscrossed with paths where, by day, locals came to walk their dogs and, by night, lonely men roamed in search of one another. Cutting through those trees, you came out on the furthest corner of the lake, where a steep wooded slope met the water's edge at a concrete storm drain.

We lay side by side on top of the outlet, watching clouds commingle, drifting together, congealing into a thick gray blanket in the sky above. We listened to the echoey drips from deep in the storm drain, the gentle lap of water against the bank. We heard, in the distance, the sound of children, playground sounds, shouts, tears. Someone paddled an inflatable dinghy at the other end of the reservoir.

"So what do they sound like?" I asked. "The voices. When you hear them."

Sylvie lay beside me so close I could almost feel her, feel her proximity like an electric current. My hand burned to reach for her, my little finger edging, edging, longing to connect. She seemed so small beside me, so compact; there was not one bit more of her than she needed, and not even that much. My fingers stretched and recoiled, daring then afraid, expanding and contracting like some skittish undersea creature; the kind of thing that dwells in shadow on the ocean floor, its hideous misshapen body an insult to nature.

"It's not a sound," Sylvie said, "so much as an . . . *everything*. An everything all at once. And all of them different. No two the same. Some smell like cold water, all silver and smoke. Some taste like rust with a shape like tree roots or seaweed. Others are all colors, all the colors all at once, only invisible, soundless, the taste of color and the smell of silence."

I laughed, not mean, just . . . bewildered. "That makes *no* sense," I said. "I don't even understand one word you just said."

"It's hard to explain," she said. "It's not like words or pictures. The room is just full of . . . of *everything*, that all-at-once everything that's a taste and a smell and a sound and then I touch it and I just know. Then it's inside me."

Above us, the clouds were thickening, the air close and metallic. From beyond the lake, the first rumble of thunder, like someone dragging a heavy box. My searching finger made contact, found the soft warmth of the edge of Sylvie's hand. I goose-pimpled, felt inside-out shivery. Sylvie snapped her head round to look at me, so quick it was like she'd been electrocuted.

"I'm sorry," I croaked and turned away, my brows knitted so tight they ached. "I didn't mean—"

Sylvie laid a hand on my chest. I glanced back and she had turned toward me, was looking right at me, unblinking. I pinched the skin of my wrist between two fingernails, pinched and pinched until the sharp pain pulled me up from the bottomless ache in my heart.

"Don't be sorry," she said. "Don't ever be sorry. You're beautiful, George. You're tree roots and fresh mown grass and the smell of rocks and apples. What's inside you is so real, so *alive*. It's burning you up."

At that moment the rumbling rolled right over us and the mountain shook with an explosion of thunder. Mist clung to the water and the first drops fell. I could see the rain across the lake like a dark curtain dragged toward us. In a moment, the air was filled with water and we were laughing and scrabbling down the side of the storm drain and into the wood, soaked through.

Sylvie ran ahead, a forest sprite flitting before me along the path. I panted behind, losing ground with each thump and slap of my feet on the sodden earth.

~

Mum wasn't sick back then. She wasn't well either, but she was still up and about most days, pottering around our place, cooking dinners, dusting shelves, making sure I was all right. I always worried when I left her alone too long.

But that day I didn't think of her at all, just followed Sylvie through the sheets of rain, through the dark of that afternoon storm, back into town and stumbling, scrabbling in through the back door of the antique shop, drenched and laughing. It was perfect. Everything about it was perfect. Sylvie's clothes clung to her, crumpled and translucent. I was shivering, but not from the cold.

She took me up the back stairs, creaky wooden steps, painted at the edges but bare in the middle where the carpet had been pulled up and never replaced. The parched wood darkened as we passed, soaked by rainwater that puddled with each footfall. At the stair-top, Sylvie pulled towels from a cupboard and pushed me into the bathroom. She locked the door behind us and began to peel away her clothes. I stood there, mute and frozen, staring as she sloughed her garments like a wet pelt, revealing goose-pimpled skin, pink from the cold. Water dripped from my pants, from my nose, from the tips of my fingers, puddled at my feet.

Sylvie stepped into the porcelain tub and drew back the curtain. Water struck the material and steam filled the room. Her silhouette turned and turned, and I imagined the water streaming down her nakedness in silvery runnels, spiraling down the plug-hole beneath her toes. She poked her head round the edge of the curtain.

"Are you going to stand there shivering all day?"

My fists clenched and unclenched. I reached a hand under my sodden top and pinched my side until the pain brought tears to my eyes, brought me back to the room. I turned away from Sylvie and began methodically to take off my clothes. I should have been cold, but I was burning, inside and out. I didn't want her to see me. My eyes stung with tears.

First, I unbuttoned then peeled away my shirt, let it drop to the floor at my feet. Then I pulled my T-shirt over my head, shrinking from the clammy feel of cotton dragged across bare skin. I unbuckled my belt and slid down my pants. They gathered around my ankles, snagged by the boots I'd forgotten to remove. I crouched awkwardly, terrified to bend, so ashamed to be this exposed, flushing so hot that the moisture came off me as steam. I pulled at the laces, ripped at the double-knot that had seemed so sensible when I'd tied them that morning.

By the time I'd tugged my jeans, all bunched and tangled, from around my ankles, Sylvie was stepping out of the shower, wrapping a towel around her. I felt a warm hand on my shoulder and shuddered.

Sylvie crouched, put her arms around me, rested her head against my shoulder blade, her hair still warm and wet from the shower.

"It's okay," she said to me, again and again. "It's okay, George. It's okay."

When I stood up, when I turned around, head drooped, so heavy with shame, burning, she didn't gasp as I'd expected. She didn't turn away. When she saw the scars, she didn't flinch. And for that I will love her forever.

Instead, she reached out to me, warm shower water still dripping from the dark tendrils of her hair. She looked up at me, looked without turning away; her brown eyes, murky pools that I felt myself falling into. I sucked in breath when she touched me, her pale bony fingertips tracing the calligraphy of half-healed cuts and gashes. The shower roared and roared. The bathroom filled with steam. When she placed a hand over my heart, I shook. And the tears would not stop.

The dryer rumbled on the other side of the attic, a dim and cluttered space, packed to overflowing with unmarked stock from the shop downstairs. We sat on tufted velvet dining chairs. I was alert and upright, clenching and unclenching my fists in my lap, while Sylvie lay semi-slumped against a mahogany dresser, her hair still wrapped in a towel. She had rummaged through an old tea chest for the clothes I now wore: a gentleman's funeral suit that pinched at the armpits, chafed at the waist and smelled strongly of mothballs and dust; still I liked the shape of it, liked the way it held me stiff and erect. A fan heater blew dry breaths toward the ceiling. The naked light bulb dangling from the rafters stirred in gentle arcs, obscure gyrations that made the shadows swell and recede.

It would be impossible to describe how I felt at that moment. Happy would be too simple. Ashamed would be unfair. Embarrassed wouldn't be the half of it. It was complicated, and it boiled within me—in the beating of my heart, in the tingling of my bare skin, in the sick heavy feeling of my body, my prison of flesh.

I reached for a silver pocket watch on the shelf beside me, held it out toward Sylvie.

"What about this one?" I asked.

Sylvie held open her hand and I lowered the watch onto her palm. She closed her eyes. The lids fluttered. "This watch was an heirloom, passed down between generations from father to son. But that's not all that was passed on. There's shame. There's disappointment, the feeling of never being good enough. The last son pawned the watch to pay for drugs."

"And this?" I passed her a toy racing car, pressed tin, burnished silver and red, with a winding key poking out the back.

"This," she said, "this was a treasure. To the boy that owned this car, it was a comfort and a friend. He kept this toy his whole life, to remind him of his mother, of his poor childhood. When he died in the nursing home, this car was his only possession."

"How about this?" I said, pointing to a navy blue commemorative tin, a scratched photo of a very young Charles and Diana.

"That one?" Sylvie said, without reaching for it. "The family that owned that one used it to store biscuits."

She laughed and I saw she was teasing. I flushed.

"You really don't feel it?" she asked. "When you touch them. You don't get that . . . taste?"

I turned an alabaster owl figurine around and around in my hands. It felt cool, smooth, heavy. I knew I liked it. I laughed and shook my head.

"To me," I said, "it's just a . . . whatever this is. It's whatever it is right now, here, with none of that other stuff."

Sylvie nodded gravely. I couldn't tell if she was disappointed or what, if I'd maybe failed some kind of test. She lay her head back down on the dresser and I noticed how careful she was to rest her hands in her lap, not touching anything around her.

I imagined running my fingertips down her bare arm, watching the skin prickle and rise.

In the corner of the attic, the dryer rattled and shook.

~

It was late when I left, and dark. I'd called Mum from the shop to let her know where I was, but I still felt guilty at having not been home to help her to bed. And the guilt was all mixed up with the confused wonder of my night with Sylvie. When the dryer finally came to a stop, I got back into my own clothes reluctantly. They seemed so baggy and formless, so wrong somehow. When I stepped outside, the streets were still soaked and steaming, though the rain had long since passed. The night was humid but not close and there was a freshness to things as of some great revelation, some buried secret brought finally to light.

The antique shop was near the center of town, just down the road from the main bus stop. There were cafés, a couple of bookshops, a designer homewares store, all for the tourists, all closed and dark. The slick wet streets distorted the night-time sounds, made them reverberate oddly, crisply. Echoes of voices in the quiet, of harsh laughter. A plume of bluish cigarette smoke rose from the bus shelter.

I crossed to the other side of the street. A can landed, clattering against the curb beside me. There were footsteps. I walked faster.

I didn't want to look around, didn't want to show my fear, but I couldn't help myself. I glanced over my shoulder and saw behind me one, two, three hooded silhouettes, quickly gaining. One of them lashed out with a foot and another can clattered, cracked against the storefront beside me. I ran, my labored, wheezing breaths loud in my ears, my heart crashing in my chest like a bursting thing. The footfalls behind me were faster, louder, gaining. I caught some movement out of the corner of my eye, and something slammed into me and I tripped, sprawled against the doorway of a darkened shop selling Italian stationery. I caught glimpses of red and orange and yellow leather, of plump round brightly colored fountain pens, before my head smashed against the door handle and I collapsed into the street. A foot swung out of the dark and into my gut. Light burst behind my eyes. I couldn't breathe.

"Well, well," said Tommy. "What have we here? A beached fucking whale."

Laughter echoed in the dead silence of the street. Darren and Boz. Distant tires on wet tarmac, out toward the highway. A mile away. An infinity.

"Get her legs," said Tommy and I was grabbed, hands, feet, dragged across the pavement and into the dark laneway.

"Fuck me," said Boz. "What a porker."

"S'all them pies," said Darren and they laughed.

"Fucking disgusting," said Tommy. He let go of my wrists and dropped me in stinking wetness. Then feet were coming from everywhere and I covered my face, curled up to protect myself.

"Pull her up," said Tommy. The kicking ceased and Darren and Boz grabbed me by the collar, yanked me upright and back against the wall, legs splayed across the filthy cobbles. My shirt ripped and I felt cold air on skin, on the raw places their feet had stomped.

"You owe us, cunt," snarled Tommy. "You fucken owe us."

"S'right," sneered Darren.

I felt so sick, I thought I'd spew. I'd been kicked so hard in so many places that nothing hurt, just burned like I was glowing, like I was on fire. My face was streaked with tears but I wasn't about to cry. It would only make it worse.

"What d'ya reckon, Tommy?" said Boz. "How'll it be to fuck The Blob?"

"Reckon you'd be lucky to find a fucken hole in that lot," said Darren and he kicked me in the side so hard I doubled over.

Tommy began to unbuckle his pants. "You know me, boys. Any hole is a goal."

I pushed myself up, back to the wall, looked up at Tommy through smeared vision. "They all tell," I said. My voice was a croak but clear enough in the quiet of the alley. "The girls. They all tell me what it's like to have sex with Tommy. They laugh when they tell me. Call you 'Tommy the Prawn.'" I waggled my little finger.

Tommy growled, smashed his fist into my nose. I heard it crunch. Fireworks exploded behind my eyes.

I forced a laugh, spat blood. "Little Tommy, they say. Little Tommy with his little prawn cocktail—"

Tommy reached into his back pocket, opened a small, mean-looking knife. The blade was viciously serrated and did not glint so much as glow. My stomach flip-flopped.

"Hold her down," he said.

I closed my eyes, clenched my teeth, knowing exactly what was about to come, how it would feel as that wicked blade sliced into me. But the hands never grabbed me. The knife never plunged. Someone was crying. And it wasn't me.

I looked up, saw Darren and Boz staggering about the alley, clutching at their heads. Tommy was on his knees, mouth gaping, staring up into the dark with rolled-back eyes. He was clawing at his face, making a gargling sound like he was choking. Then Boz was yelling, smashing at his head with his palms. Darren wailed, ran off down the alley toward the street.

Silhouetted against the orange streetlights, Sylvie stood in the alley mouth. Her hands were thrust down at her sides, balled into fists. She didn't move, didn't flinch as first Darren, then Boz, tripped past her, bounced off the walls and into the street, tearing at their hair.

Sylvie moved toward Tommy, her steps slow and measured. Tommy was blubbering. He whimpered. As Sylvie approached, he writhed, convulsing, pressing his fingers so deep into his temples, into the sockets of his eyes, that the tips disappeared. He looked like he was trying to tear his face from his skull.

Sylvie's face was in darkness, her eyes shadowed. Perhaps it was a trick of the streetlights, of the moisture in the air, but the last thing I remember seeing was a kind of halo around her head.

No. Not a halo. More like a crown. A crown of snakes, of black smoke that poured from her head and into Tommy, twitching on the wet cobbles of the alley.

EPISODIAE

At the end of that summer, Sylvie left for university; not down in the city, as I'd hoped, but out of state. Saying goodbye hollowed me out inside.

I was going to go too, to uni that is—I had the grades, had put in applications. But Mum got really sick, a stroke that paralyzed her all down the right side, left her face droopy and slack. Her words came out like she'd just been to the dentist. There was no way she could take care of herself and no one else to take care of her, so I stayed home, got a job nearby.

I got a job, in fact, working with Sylvie's dad in the antique shop. I'd wanted to work at the library but, even though I'd been sorting books at school since forever, you needed a degree to apply; even if I'd had the degree, the mountains had just the one library and they weren't hiring. But working for Christophe was okay. The pay wasn't great, but he was kind to me and in my lunch breaks I could walk home to check on Mum. On the caregiver's day off, I wheeled her in to sit with me in the shop, just for the change of scene.

Christophe knew I wasn't so into the front-of-house stuff, so he gave me free rein to work in the back rooms, or up in the attic, sorting through all the objects. He let me bring some order to that whimsical chaos. I spent long afternoons grouping artifacts, cataloging them, pricing. The attic had a skylight I'd never noticed when I'd been there with Sylvie, and murky daylight streamed through it, onto ancient leather sofas and teak cabinets, onto andirons and ottomans. Sometimes it rained and the attic became an eerie gray space, blanketed by the sounds of pelting water, of streaming gutters. When it rained I thought of Sylvie and ached.

Christophe was a quiet, gentle man. I think he liked me because I was Sylvie's friend. He trusted me to just get on and do my thing, while he craned over the heavy leather desk near the front of the shop, worrying away at his notes, with one or another fusty leather-bound book spread open in front of him. On the desk, beside the antique till and the photo of Sophie's mum, was a bust of some old guy. I'd thought it was Christophe, as it looked so much like him—the sad eyes, the almost smile, the full beard and lank long hair—but it turned out to be a plaster replica of a real sculpture from ancient Greece. That desk was forever strewn with loose papers, each one blackened with Christophe's illegible scrawl. For the better part of every working day he sat stooped over that desk, his eyebrows bundled, finger tracing the lines of figures in whichever bygone tome, ignoring the *dingaling* of the bell on the rare occasions a customer did come in.

But we got on well enough, I suppose. Perhaps because, no matter how different we were, we always had that one thing in common—we both missed Sylvie, both felt her absence like a ragged hole.

Sylvie's mum—where she was, what had happened to her—never came up. Sylvie had never spoken of her, except in the vaguest terms. I assumed she had died, but neither Sylvie nor Christophe ever told me one way or the other. The only trace of her seemed to be that sad-looking black-and-white photo on the edge of Christophe's desk.

I spent most of my time at the shop in the attic, but at lunchtime Christophe would head out. He'd shuffle all the papers into a bundle and use a stack of books as a paperweight to hold them in place. He'd roll himself a cigarette and stroll off down the main street, trailing plumes of foul-smelling smoke. Every day, he took his lunch at the same café, smoked one cigarette on the way there, another on the way back. While he was out, I'd sit at the desk. The chair was a wood and leather swivel job, uncomfortably small. Squeezing myself into it, inhaling the fug of stale tobacco and old paper, made me feel like I was someone else, a ghost inside a stranger's body.

Other times, I'd wander round the shop, remembering the stories Sylvie had told me about the objects there. I'd brush my fingers against them as she had, or pick them up from where they lay, cradling them against the meat of my palm. But they never spoke to me. All I felt was cool porcelain, burnished metal, polished wood. They were what they were, what my eyes told me they were. Never more, never less. The only ghost that ever spoke to me was the ghost of Sylvie, the sadness that came to me whenever I was reminded of her, as I always was. I couldn't escape her memory and I wanted it that way, to be always surrounded by her, by the things she had touched and known. To keep that pain forever keen.

~

I didn't think back often to that night. Not on purpose anyway. It surfaced sometimes, as cruel memories often will, unexpected and with force. Those flashes, when they came, were worst when I was home, awake and alone after putting Mum to bed. At the shop, it was different. I felt . . . protected somehow. Perhaps because, there, my thoughts were forever on Sylvie, so when I flashed back to that night and Tommy standing over me, the memory was always of her, silhouetted in the alley, the boys running in fear, the black shadows coiling around her. I remembered how she had taken care of me, rode with me in the ambulance, how she told the paramedic I was her sister. She sat with me late into that night, long after exhaustion and whatever they'd given me for the pain had dragged me into sleep.

When I awoke, bound and aching, with broken nose, broken

ribs, everywhere as stiff and sore as if I'd tumbled down the mountain, Sylvie was gone and two police officers were in the room. The woman sat erect in the visitor's chair, her hat on the table next to the water jug and tumbler, her hands resting discreetly against a black leather pad in her lap. Behind her stood the man, hat on, with hands behind his back, as stiff as a soldier. When she saw I was awake, the woman turned to the man, who nodded, left the room without a word and closed the door behind him.

She turned back to me and smiled. "Now it's just us girls," she said and I bristled. The interview went downhill from there.

Maybe because I was groggy from all the drugs, or cranky from the dully blooming pain, but everything about Constable 'Call me Tanya' Bale irked me. I suppose she was just doing her job, trying to be sympathetic, to put me at ease. But, instead, she came across as patronizing, overfamiliar, calling me again and again by my hated name. At one point I got so angry that I clenched my teeth and the fractures in my skull flared. When I turned away with tears in my eyes, she thought I was reliving the trauma or something, told me there was nothing to be afraid of, that I was safe here. I just wanted her gone.

"It was dark," I said. "It happened so fast. I didn't get a good look at any of them."

She gave me a look brimming with disappointment, angry almost. Like I was the one at fault.

"I'm sorry," I said.

"*You* have nothing to be sorry for, Georgina," she said. The smile she gave me was so pinched it looked as if she was actually biting her tongue, having to hold in what she really thought of me, what she really wanted to say.

When Sylvie came by again that afternoon, she'd brought grapes and we both laughed. I was too sore to eat, but she perched on the edge of the chair beside the bed, eating grape after grape. She talked to me through mouthfuls with her lips pushed forward in a funny pout, her eyes wide and excitable. I'd never seen her so lively. Her hand resting on mine looked so tiny and white, like a porcelain doll's. But at one point, as if to emphasize what she was saying, she squeezed my hand so hard I gasped. She laughed, but it wasn't mean or awkward. When she laughed at me, the look she gave me, I felt that she *knew* me, knew *me*, in a way that no one else ever had, or had ever even tried to.

"How did you know?" I asked. "How did you know to come, where to find me?"

"They told me," she said. And though I didn't understand, I didn't press it further.

~

In that first year Sylvie was away, I started going to a mixed martial arts class. The dojo was a ten-minute walk from the shop, just across the train tracks in North Blackworth. Every Monday and Thursday, I'd walk straight from work to wrap myself in a *gi* and tie on the white belt.

I felt ridiculous at first. Lumbering around the mat, sweating my clothes dark throwing punches and kicks—*one two three four five six seven eight nine ten, now swap*. Then holding the pads for someone better than me to throw punches and kicks at. Being flung this way and that, feeling the room shake whenever I fell. But I persisted. I realized I didn't care what anyone thought, that I wanted this. I'd weather the teasing and the whispered jokes and always being picked last—though the sensei cut all of that short quick enough, doling out push-ups left and right. I liked how the training made me feel, the way it burned and exhausted my limbs, punished my body, brought it back in line. I trained because I wanted to. It had nothing to do with what had happened that night.

I thought often of Tommy standing over me, folding open that wicked looking knife. Every time I remembered it, I'd start to sweat and my heart would pound just the same as it did right there in the alley. But it made no sense to me, this fear. I knew all too clearly just how it would feel, that knife, as it sliced. In my own hands I would not have feared it, would have treasured it, even, made a special place for it in my secret tin. It wasn't the knife I feared, or the pain. I wasn't even afraid of Tommy, not really. It was the helplessness. The lack of control.

In those first months, as I threw myself more deeply into the training, I took the old tin out from its hiding place less and less, the need for my treasures receding like a hunger now sated.

Sylvie came home every holiday, back to the mountains. The weeks before she returned were always tense for me and Christophe, as though both of us were fighting to contain our excitement. I'd spend long hours in the attic, half-sprawled on the leather couch, fingering the doodads on an old charm bracelet, or toying with a dark wooden puzzle box, needing something to do with my hands while I stared through the skylight, eyes drawn to the blanket of thick gray, or the passage of lone puffs of cloud in an otherwise unspoiled blue. Whenever I came downstairs to the shop, I'd find Christophe bumbling, his notes forgotten, sorting through piles of books he'd already priced, or rolling cigarettes to tuck behind his ear, only to find one already there. We never snapped at each other, but we were both out of sorts, like the heaviness in summer before a storm breaks.

When she did return, it was so awkward, Christophe could barely contain himself and Sylvie seemed overwhelmed. I hung back, not wanting to put myself in the picture, no matter how desperate I was to be close to Sylvie, to feel her fingers brush my arm.

But something wasn't right. The first days back she seemed a different person. Her posture was somehow changed, her eyes were more searching, less dreamy. She had an accent that wasn't her own. Even the things she talked about seemed alien, not things that *my* Sylvie would be interested in. It never lasted though. That excitement, that alienness, was like a skin she wore, a kind of protective armor that fell away in scales the longer she was home. She was never truly herself until she'd spent time alone in the attic.

That first holiday, I came in for work, climbed the creaky stairs to find Sylvie perched on the edge of the chair she'd sat on that night, as we'd waited for our clothes to dry. Her head was drooped, hair hanging like a chestnut waterfall. She looked up when I came in and I saw her eyes were ringed with red. She smiled; and it was the smile I knew, alive with deep sadness. Resting on her lap was the silver-framed photograph of her mother. As I lowered myself into the couch across from her, she lifted her fingers from the frame, as though breaking a silent and invisible connection. She placed the photograph on the dresser beside her, face down. From that moment until the next term began, she was entirely herself.

Each time the holidays rolled around and Sylvie returned, I found it harder and harder to bear that armored Sylvie, the Sylvie of the first days who was not the person I knew and who kept me at a distance. I grew impatient with her, wanted the change to be instantaneous, for her to be herself from the first moment I saw her. I conspired to get her into the attic sooner and sooner after she arrived, grew frustrated when she resisted. It was like she didn't want to be herself. Like she didn't want to be my friend.

Whenever she was away, I longed for her return, but when she was back, it hurt so much I couldn't bear it. I was so happy to be near her, to hear her voice bubbling, to pretend to her and myself that I wasn't falling into the deep wide black of her eyes. And yet, the closer we were and the happier I felt, the more painful it was, the more unbearable, as though her proximity was the very thing that separated us, that drove her further from me. The Sylvie I pined for in her absence was always herself, always the Sylvie I needed her to be. In my dreams and longing, I could imagine us together, forever entwined, an intimacy tinged with beautiful sadness. I imagined her fingers brushing my arms, tracing the scars along my belly and breasts, my own hands, huge against her slightness, marking the shapes of her delicate body. I imagined us laying together in the attic with the rain hammering against the skylight, falling in sheets from the overflowing drainpipes.

But the Sylvie that returned each time, though more beautiful than the faceless porcelain doll of my fantasies, was more complicated, more troubled, more distant. When I was with her, my hands lay in my lap, balled into fists so tight that my knuckles ached. At night, after Mum was tucked up in bed, I'd shut myself in the bathroom, pull back that loose tile. I'd carve into my body another line in the epic poem of my heart's pain, of my weightless ghost imprisoned within its mountain of flesh.

As the summer neared, I vowed to myself for the millionth time that I would tell her what was in my heart. I imagined her rejection over and over, believing that the pain of it could not compare to the pain I already felt, living the lie of her friend but nothing more. And for the millionth time I would rage at myself, at my selfishness, my stupidity, at the longing that, if released, would surely tear apart everything that meant anything to me. So I went back and forth, talking myself in and out of baring my soul to her, of risking everything on a chance to make her mine.

But that summer, when Sylvie returned, she was not alone.

I disliked Dane from the moment Sylvie introduced him. He exuded a kind of bombastic confidence, a blusterous positivity I couldn't stand and couldn't believe in.

Dane was a business major, studying financial economics. He was two years ahead of Sylvie and a full two heads taller, with an iron-backed erectness that I resented immediately. I was taller still, of course, or would have been if I'd ever stood straight. But no one was allowed to be better than Dane, in anything—he had to be the best and brightest, the most successful, the most buff. Dane spent two hours every morning at the gym, lived off protein supplements and muesli bars and drank milk in such quantities it nauseated me.

When he first came into the shop, Dane swaggered over to the display cases, cast an appraising eye over their contents and picked from a nearby table an ornate French Empire bronze urn, gilded with ormolu. He turned it over in his hands, oblivious to Christophe's sharp intake of breath, weighing it like a piece of meat in a butcher's shop. "This worth much?" he said. Continuing his audit of the shop's gross value, he perused his way over to the shelves on the far wall, row upon row of books from other centuries, with spines of fabric and leather embossed with gold leaf. He turned back to Christophe and called, "You got any biographies? I only read biographies."

I could see Christophe was as much taken aback by this visitor as I was. When the offered hand was shaken vigorously by Dane, I saw the older man wince behind a forced smile. I knew he was wondering how long he was expected to endure the presence of this unwanted guest.

Sylvie was entirely out of sorts, not herself at all. Beside Dane, she stood sheepishly, awkward in her own body in a way I'd never seen. She laughed too hard at Dane's dull jokes and giggled like a child whenever he pulled her toward him with those possessive hands. I couldn't get a second alone with her. Dane was *always* there. I had to follow her to the toilet to have even one word in private.

"I thought maybe we could catch up tomorrow," I said. "Just

you and me. Go down to the outlet and hang by the lake. Like we used to. The weather's supposed to be nice."

"Oh," she said and puffed out her lips; the expression didn't suit her at all, made a mannequin of that face once so alive with sadness. "Oh George, you sweet thing. I would *love* to do that, but I already said I'd spend the morning with Dane."

I tried not to let the hurt show, pushed it down to smolder deep inside me with all the rest of my anger. But it must have glowed in my eyes or pulled at the corners of my mouth, because Sylvie softened, or seemed too.

"Oh George," she said and touched my arm with a sympathy that almost passed as sincere. "We will catch up soon, I promise. It's just this is Dane's first time here and I want to show him around. And I want him to get to know you too, and for you to know him. I'm sure you'll get on so well . . ."

The next day was my day off. I was so angry, so burningly jealous of Dane, of the way Sylvie looked at him, his stupid chiseled features, his athlete's body, his roaming hands and the ease with which they laid claim to Sylvie. It all made me burn so hot I couldn't bear to be near them. I walked out to the edge of town, out through the forest path and down to the edge of the lake. But before I came to the place where the trees thinned, opened out onto the lake's muddy banks bristling with rushes, I heard voices. Foolish, girlish giggling. The brash, confident tones of a young man. Sylvie. And Dane.

I followed the tree line round, willing my footfalls to be light, my bulk to disappear. I watched them through the yellow dust of acacia blooms. They lay on the concrete outlet, sun-baking. Dane wore nothing on top and Sylvie's small white hand brushed his bare chest with gentle strokes. My stomach convulsed. I bit down so hard on the flesh of my finger that my teeth broke the skin.

I trained all afternoon, in the back room of the dojo while classes ran in the hall. I beat at the punchbag, smashing it over and over with fists clenched so tight I felt the bones would break.

The bag swung and swung and I pounded and punched, grunting and sweating. By the time I went home to cook dinner for Mum, my body ached all over and my knuckles were raw. But though the pain helped bring me back, helped rein in the disgust that crawled through my flesh like an infection, it did nothing to touch that deep burning rage.

That night, after I'd tucked Mum into bed, I took out my old tobacco tin from its hiding place and shut myself in the bathroom. For the first time in months, I took out my treasures, one by one, and laid them along the edge of the bath, their sharpness glinting in the cool fluorescence.

I closed my eyes and pressed down on the blade, enslaving that chaos of emotion to a single brilliant point of control.

~

Christophe had expected Sylvie to stay until term began, but, after only a few days, Dane left and Sylvie went with him. In the long summer weeks that followed, his lunchtime walks took longer than usual. When he came back, he smelled not only of tobacco smoke but of wine. His eyes were heavy and sad. He let customers talk him into outrageous discounts, as though he had lost all sense of the value of things.

He told me about the day Sylvie left. Dane had been out since early morning, running around the lake, working out at the gym. Sylvie had taken the silver-framed portrait up to the attic. When Dane returned, he found her there, weeping. Christophe heard them, heard Dane yell, "I don't like things that make you cry." He snatched the photo from her and in the struggle it fell. The glass inside the frame broke.

"Jesus, Sylvie," Dane had said. "You're really bringing me down. This place is bad for you, all this sadness. You need to just let it go, get on with your life."

I wasn't working the day they left, so didn't get to see her or even say goodbye. When I came in on the Monday, she was gone.

～

I hoped that Dane was just a passing thing, a first-year fling that would be over in months. I pictured Sylvie abandoned, her eyes red and raw from tears. I pictured my palm cupping Sylvie's cheek, my thumb stroking the salty wetness that streaked her face. I imagined the taste of her tears, the feel of her small tongue as it pressed its way into my mouth, parting my lips with earnest, probing movements. I dreamed how it would feel to lie, her small pale body pressed against mine, we two, clothed in nothing but scars and sadness.

Toward the end of summer, I wrote a letter. I wrote everything that was in my heart, my anger, my love, my distrust of Dane. It felt good to put it all down on paper like that, my forefingers aching from holding the pen. But when I read it through, I knew I couldn't send it. I tried to rewrite it, to make it less raw, less open, less like a great gaping wound that I was baring just for her. But, no matter how I tried, the words wouldn't come right. To tell it any other way was a lie.

I tore at those pages until they were just tiny scraps, until the pieces covered my bed like the dust of some forgotten, unreclaimable time.

EXODOS

Sylvie had been away close on two years when Mum died.

It wasn't exactly out of the blue, still it came as a shock. She'd been doing so well, was getting movement back in her right side, had regained enough control to scratch a child's scrawl of her name on the handful of Christmas cards she sent out each year. But the summer was a hot one—on some days well into the forties—and maybe it was the heat, or maybe it was something else, but a week after New Year's she had another stroke. I rode with her in the ambulance, held her hand under the blanket, under the straps. All those tubes and wires... The oxygen pump gasped. Machines beeped. Her hand went limp. She was dead before we even made it to the hospital.

The funeral was small, depressing. Only a handful of people came: Mum's sister Geraldine and her husband; the caregiver who'd helped me with Mum since her first stroke; Christophe. It was held at the North Blackworth Crematorium, over on the other side of the highway. The gardens were nice enough, I suppose, but the church seemed phony, with its cheap curtains and rows of uncomfortable chairs. Even the flowers looked plastic. The priest said all kinds of rubbish about Mum, a whole load of made-up rubbish about what a good Christian she was, though Mum never believed any of that hoo-ha. There was something so pitiful about the coffin, trundling back through the curtain, and the music, tinny and grating through the small, dusty speakers.

I wore a black suit I'd picked up at Vinnies. It was extra, extra large, but sat funny on me even still; pinched in places, bagged in others. It didn't look funereal so much as criminal. With my hair slicked back and down I looked like a bouncer, or a hoodlum from a gangster movie. It was so uncomfortable, I kept shifting and shuffling about, making the chair creak. I could feel sweat soaking into the underarms of the new white shirt.

I gave the eulogy. It was me that knew Mum best, but still it wasn't all that good. I didn't know what to say and just felt daft, stood at the front of that echoey room, almost empty. How could you sum up a life—a whole life—with just a few words? How could you even try? No one knew her better than me, but even I only knew her from the outside. Who could say what was underneath, what luminous ghost struggled beneath those layers of flesh, the body that resisted her control and had been for so many years her enemy.

Everyone came back to the house after. I'd bought wine and crackers and cheese. Geraldine poked around the house looking for things to steal, sore that Mum had left it all to me. She got drunk and snide, speaking down to me in her cruel and whiny voice as if I were a child.

"Whatever happened to you, Georgina?" Geraldine slurred, her eyes fogged and droopy. "You were such a pretty little thing. Always a bit on the chubby side, I'll grant. But you had such a smile. So pretty. Whatever happened?"

"Come on, Geraldine," said her husband, whose name I could never remember, Grant or Gary or Greg. "Leave her alone."

"*You* leave her alone," spat the drunken old witch. "What happened, girl? Just look at you. Like a brick shit-house and all dressed up like a fucking bloke. What must your mum have thought, you growing up into a bloody great—"

"That'll do," said Greg or Gary or Grant, and he and Christophe took her, one to an arm, and pulled her toward the door. "Let's get you in the car."

"Thank you, George," he said over his shoulder. "Sorry about your mum. She was a good sort."

That night, after I'd cleaned away the empty bottles, the paper cups and plates and all the detritus of the wake, I sat in my undies looking down at the old tobacco tin, at my treasures all laid out on the edge of the bath. I must have sat like that an hour or more, just staring down at them glinting there, before I picked them up one by one and packed them away.

Sylvie hardly came back at all that summer. Christophe got a postcard to say that she and Dane had gone to the Great Barrier Reef, some kind of diving adventure holiday. It didn't sound like the sort of thing Sylvie would have been into. When she finally returned at the end of the summer, she was so happy it was absurd. She was almost unrecognizable.

I was in the attic when she bounded up the creaking stairs, swanning round the place like she owned it. I was preoccupied, wrapped up in Mum being gone, in sorting out her estate—Geraldine was contesting the Will, trying to get her hands on the house. I had a lot on my plate at the shop, too, and didn't have time for this new Sylvie, with her cardboard cut-out joie de vivre and patchwork of self-help economics and popular psychology. Who even was this person? I felt I didn't know her at all.

"You look smart," she said, sidling toward me through stacks of unpriced furniture with a poise that made me hate her.

I'd taken to wearing a suit every day, ever since Mum's funeral.

Mostly second-hand numbers I picked up in thrift stores and flea markets, adjusted to my size by Mrs. Nguyen round the corner. It felt right, but I was still self-conscious.

I grunted, gave a nod, pretending not to look up from the French sorcière mirror I was turning over and over in my hands. My fingertips began to sweat.

"It suits you," she said. "Very . . . contained."

"How was your trip?" I asked without looking up. I didn't want to know, didn't want to be making small talk like this, pretending. I didn't want to hear about Dane. The attic felt stuffy, the collar of my shirt too tight.

"Wonderful," she said in an affected drawl that didn't suit her. "I've never seen an ocean so blue. And turtles. Turtles and rays and so many brightly colored fish, I couldn't begin to name them all. It was magnificent."

As she talked, she twirled slowly, taking in the many shelves of objects, some I had already sorted, with paper price tags dangling by a thread, others yet to be appraised, languishing in boxes and tea chests, stacked one upon the other against the attic wall.

"Yes, it was splendid. And most wonderful of all was who we met while we were out there. A chance in a million. You'll simply never believe it."

I made a noise, investing as much effort as my level of interest would allow, all the while buffing at the convex mirror in my hands, wiping away the dust from the carved wooden leaves surrounding it.

Sylvie had stopped beside an unrestored dresser, leaned forward to examine a porcelain figurine, a sleeping nude in a bed of flowers. "Yes," she said. "The most wonderful doctor. Swiss, I think, or maybe Austrian. A specialist."

I saw her reach for the figurine. Her fingers opened to receive it and I looked up from what I was doing, the mirror forgotten in my hands.

"A specialist?" The words came out, but it was as if they had nowhere to go; they hung there between us like a frozen breath.

"An expert," she said and reached until her fingers were so close they might almost have brushed the nude. "Someone qualified to deal with my little . . . problem."

She hesitated and her fingers drew back.

I was so stunned, I didn't know what to say. There was something in her eyes, then, like the old sadness, a glimmer of something real and true and alive. The Sylvie I used to know.

There was something else, too, in the look she gave me. Fear, perhaps. Or despair. For a moment it seemed she might collapse, sobbing into my lap, plead with me to rescue her.

But then she forced a smile and the mask came down, and she turned and left the attic without another word.

～

The next year, Sylvie didn't come back at all. Christophe went out of state for her graduation, left me in charge of the shop. When he returned, he looked older somehow. Weighed down. Sylvie wasn't coming home.

That was the year I got my brown belt. I was training every day then, pounding the bag in the back room. All that exercise had changed me. It's not that I'd lost weight or anything, but I was solid; when I washed the sweat from myself in the shower back home, the water coursed over scars stretched tight with muscle.

Boz joined the dojo that year. He did a double take to see me, demonstrating moves with the sensei, training the white belts. When it came to his turn, he looked this way and that, trying to catch the eye of any other trainer. But there was only me. He looked straight-up petrified when I beckoned him with a gesture of my hand. I thought it would be weird, him being there, but it wasn't. I hardly ever thought of that night anymore. When I grabbed him by the collars, rolled him back and over, came down on top of him with my knees pinning his arms, it was strictly professional. The anger just wasn't there.

Darren was doing well, I'd heard. Assistant manager at the local Office Works. Someone told me he and Tansy Rimer were together now, that he'd bought her a sparkly ring. "Next there'll be wedding bells," they'd said and I shrugged. Signing the papers down at the local council wasn't exactly "wedding bells." And what did I care about those old bullies, when school already seemed so long ago, like the distant past.

Things were harder for Tommy. I saw him one time, crossing the highway over by the old courthouse, looking scrawny as a chicken. He was sucking on a cigarette so hard it caved his cheeks in, waiting at the lights with a girl no more than sixteen. She had sunken eyes and her mascara was black and smeared and made her look like a skeleton; a skeleton in black leggings and pink Ugg boots. While Tommy smoked, walking just in front of her, the skeleton girl pushed the stroller. Tommy was yelling something at the girl. The baby screamed and screamed.

Every night I trained. Every night I came home to the empty house. My days were all about the shop. I'd learned a fair bit about antiques in the time I'd been working there, enough for me to drive out in Christophe's old van in search of new treasures, touring the antique fairs and estate sales. I always came back with something good, sometimes with a haul. In between times, I'd built us a website, started buying and selling pieces online. I worked every day of the week.

I'd moved into Mum's bedroom with the built-in wardrobe and was stocking it slowly but surely with quality vintage garments. I started picking them up when I did my weekday rounds of the markets. Suits my size weren't easy to come by, but I'd found a few beauties on my travels: double-breasted flannel, deep navy worsted, and my weekend favorite, Harris Tweed. Half the wardrobe hung with crisp shirts in muted colors, cut to exactly my size by Mrs. Nguyen's expert hands.

Christophe still sat each day at the front desk, still had his smoke and his stroll. Only now, we'd close up the shop for lunch and walk down the street together: Christophe, puffing at his disgusting roll-up; me, balling and releasing my fists, feeling all that caged power. We'd sit side by side in the dim café Christophe had come to every day since he first moved to town with Sylvie. We'd eat without speaking, at peace in the hubbub of others' conversations. In the years we'd been working together, I'd grown to love him in the way of an uncle or a father. A quiet way that grew out of our long, shared silences, from the many hundreds of hours watching him potter through his routine, pining for Sylvie in his own fashion, much as I pined for her in mine. We always had that, the unspoken bond between us, the love of our lives that had rejected us both.

On his desk still sat the ancient till, the fake marble bust, and beside them the silver-framed photograph. But there was another picture on the desk now, in a delicate marquetry frame of pale and dark wood—a black-and-white portrait of Sylvie. It was taken the year before she went to university. Her smile was crooked. Her eyes wide and filled with sadness.

∿

I'd given up all hope of seeing Sylvie again, resigned myself to the choice she'd made, her life with Dane and the person she'd become. The rawness of my love had scabbed and healed over. All that remained was the scar. And the nagging, persistent itch buried too deep to be relieved.

But then the postcard arrived from Switzerland. The photo showed peaks of white capped mountains in the background, rolling verdant hills and a lake as blue and still as polished glass. In the foreground, two girls in traditional Swiss dress sat beside each other on the meadow. Both girls were looking straight at the camera, their eyes the same brilliant blue as the lake.

I stood for a long time staring at that picture, not daring to turn over the card to see what was written on the back. My heart trembled in its cage of meat and bone.

Darling G,

I saw this card and thought of you. Two girls at the lake (but no rain this time). I hope father is treating you well. I'll be home this summer to see you both. I have such wonderful news!

Your S

My legs went so limp I had to sit down at the kitchen table. I read and re-read those words, trying to make sense of them.

Darling G . . . Your S

It had been years since Sylvie wrote to me, even a few words, and never with such intimacy. It made me so excited I thought I'd be sick. I could hardly sleep that night for thinking of it, what it might mean.

Each morning, when I woke, the postcard was the first thing I reached for. When I dressed to go to the shop, I tucked it into the inside pocket of that morning's suit, holding it close to my breast, to my pounding heart. When I got home each evening, when I changed for training, I slipped it from the pocket, read it again, before propping it against the bedroom mirror. In bed, I read it one last time, fell asleep with it under my pillow, my fingers brushing the place where she had, at last, revealed the secrets of her heart.

Your S

I had forgotten entirely what she told me in the attic, didn't make the connection—the significance of Switzerland. I had forgotten all about the "specialist." I was so consumed by the flame that postcard had ignited that I imagined "wonderful news" could mean only one thing: that Sylvie had finished with Dane and was coming home.

To me.

~

The morning of Sylvie's arrival, I wore my best suit: a vintage Kiton cashmere, with wide lapels and a Glen check. It had cost a fortune, but that seemed a small price for how I felt inside it, how well it hung against my now-muscular form. I'd sat up half the night polishing a pair of brown-and-white two-tone wingtips that gleamed on my feet. I slicked my hair, checked my reflection in the mirror. I had never in my life looked so entirely like myself.

The *dingaling* of the bell, as I pushed open the door to the shop, was so cheerful that morning, so filled with the promise of a lifetime's hopes realized at last. Christophe greeted me with a nod as I entered. He looked exhausted, leaning on the edge of his desk as though he'd aged overnight. His brow was wrinkled, mouth pinched, his expression strained. I pulled a face, began to ask him what was the matter, but before I could speak, I heard footsteps pattering down the wooden stairs and there was Sylvie.

I smoothed back my hair from its parting, stood into my full height.

"George," she said, crossing the floor. "You look . . . incredible. It's been too long."

She looked more beautiful than I had ever remembered. Her

dark hair spilled like feathers around her bare shoulders and down the back of a cream A-line frock. Her mouth, when she spoke, was so small, so perfect, like a ripe raspberry. My body was going haywire at the sight of her, melting and exploding and dissolving and electric all at once. I could already imagine the feel of her pressed against me, wrinkling the lines of my suit.

As she glided toward me between the stacked bookshelves, past the wall of softly ticking clocks, the glass display case of Victorian wind-up toys and through the labyrinth of restored antique furniture, her fingers brushed the objects. Her hands made lithe motions, almost dancing, just as they had in the attic of my memory, when she had tasted the ghosts of each object's past with her feather-light touch. It was Sylvie as I had always remembered her.

Only it wasn't.

The movements were the same, the gestures identical. But her face, her eyes. The attention she held on me was entirely wrong, the smile fixed and meaningless. And her eyes. Her eyes did not waver. The lids did not once flutter.

She embraced me and I stiffened. Every nerve ending aflame. Wanting to give everything to her, but knowing this was *not* Sylvie.

"I'm so glad you're here, my darling," she said. "It's so wonderful. So perfect."

There came a sound of thunder from above, heavy boots on hollow wood. Dane burst into the room.

"There you are," he said. "And about time."

"Oh George," said Sylvie and beamed at me with perfect artifice.

"Sylvie and I—" said Dane.

My heart was convulsing with such force I thought the buttons on my shirt would split.

"Sylvie's going to be my wife."

Christophe turned to me, his eyes clouded with pain.

～

The day was interminable. Sylvie and Dane invited us to lunch to celebrate their "wonderful" news. Christophe closed the shop for the afternoon.

We drove all together in Dane's Lexus, up the mountain to Le Sommet, a stuffily pretentious restaurant on the view side of the mountains' most expensive hotel. Known by locals to be overpriced, understaffed and overrated, the place was kept alive by romantic city weekenders and the endless busloads of Asian tourists. It reminded me in many ways of Dane—showy and characterless, its surface glamor barely concealing a mania for acquisition and wealth.

Dane spared no expense. A window seat, the set menu, a bottle of Krug waiting in a bucket of ice. The pop of the cork, the tinkle of the glasses, the spritzing effervescence of the bubbles, all assaulted me with their refinement. Each sip was like poison. Dane blathered on and on. Sylvie showed off her ring, beamed vapidly. Christophe sat rigid, forking up that posh food with awkward movements, washing it all down with far too much wine. I was too stunned to speak. I didn't know what to do with myself, didn't understand what I was doing there.

We were the only patrons in the restaurant that afternoon. Just us, the waiter and the in-house performer. The empty room echoed with overloud ballads played on a grand piano so shiny-white it looked cheap—Elton John, Neil Diamond, Engelbert Humperdinck.

The afternoon wore on with no hope of an end. I watched Sylvie from across the table—her facile expression, her learned gestures—my heart as dull and heavy as a punching bag. I played and replayed our last moments in the shop together. Christophe had gone upstairs for his coat and Dane was bringing the car around. Sylvie and I stood by the front desk. I hadn't known what to say, couldn't bear to open myself to this Sylvie I didn't recognize or understand. I stood stiffly, fists balled.

She was talking at me, a shower of sparkly patter that I registered only as sound. As she spoke, she moved things around on the desk, picking them up, putting them down. She turned the silver-framed photograph toward her, lifted it from the desk and looked for a long time at the picture of her mother, fingering the pattern of grooves around the edge of the frame.

Then she looked up from the portrait and smiled at me, placed it back on the desk just as she had found it. Her expression—the look in her eyes—had not changed, as though she had felt nothing at that old, familiar contact.

Nothing at all.

It was dark when the taxi dropped us back at the shop and a murky fluorescence pooled beneath the streetlights. The temperature had dropped and mist curled in the cab's blue-white beams. I felt drunk, though I'd hardly sipped at the champagne. I should have gone to training, but went, instead, straight home and locked the door behind me.

All the lights were off and I felt my way up the stairs, shedding clothes as I climbed. The suit jacket fell by the front door in a heap, the tie at the foot of the stairs. The cufflinks plinked and plunked on the risers as the dress shirt sloughed away like an unwanted skin. By the time I reached the bathroom, fumbled for the light switch, I wore only my undies.

I ripped at the loose tile beneath the bath and pulled out the old tobacco tin, laid out all my treasures one by one. They sparkled, brilliant in their sharpness. Each blade sang its own melody—songs of metal and flesh, of the gleaming knife edge between the body's end and the soul's beginning. The scars on my arms and chest and thighs chorused in harmony. The vibrations were so intense I felt they might tear me apart.

My hand hovered for what seemed an age, tuning in to the magnetic resonance of each precious treasure, seeking that frequency most in tune with my heart's own mournful contralto. My fingers closed around the old school compass, the one that had lain in the dark corners of my pencil case since the sixth grade. I savored the coldness of the metal, the weathered black plastic, the savage gleaming point. I pressed down, shuddered as the tip sank into the muscle above my knee, moaned as my hand moved back, dragging the point through thigh flesh, carving a track all the way to my groin. My eyes were filled with tears. My scars buzzed. The cut was ragged and profane, the edges curled back from glistening red meat.

I passed the compass to my left hand.

Choking a sob, I raked the point from my other knee to the cleft of my thigh. The compass fell to the tiles with a clatter. Spots of red gleamed on shining white. The sound of dripping, like a tap not fully closed.

I reached out again for my treasures. My fingers, shaking now, brushed first against the rough hasp of the scalpel, next against the machined grooves of an unsheathed razor blade. It was a decision won by feel. I gripped the scalpel handle, pressed my thumb down on the base, the blade jutting beneath my fist. I lay an arm upon my bloody thigh, palm up. My fingers clenched and unclenched, like a dying spider.

I didn't press, at first. Instead, I let the point of the scalpel rest against the soft tent of skin between the tendons of my wrist. I didn't press, just let the weight of the handle sink the blade. When the skin broke, I gasped. My eyes squeezed tears. I clenched my teeth, exhaling with a groan, pushed down. The blade sank so deep it scraped bone. Panting, sobbing, I dragged back and down, pressing and dragging and wailing. And though the muscles around each fissure throbbed and howled and every severed nerve shrieked, it was not enough to draw me away from that deeper pain, the sorrow that no blade could reach because it was not in my body. I shook with sobs.

When I switched the scalpel to my left hand, I could barely close my fist; only my first and little fingers would bend enough to clutch it, and the handle was now so sticky and wet that it slipped and slid. When I tightened my grip, blood waterfalled from the furrow. The groove I cut into my right arm was less deep, but more jagged, took much, much longer to complete. Each beat of my heart made a swirling, whooshing sound, so loud in my ears.

I never did manage to pick up the razor. The scalpel fell, clattered distantly, as though rebounding from the walls of a very deep, very resonant well. I pitched forward from the toilet seat into a spreading pool of myself.

I was gone before my forehead struck the tiles.

~

And then...

~

What happened after, I've never told anyone. Not even Christophe—who I trust, perhaps, more than anyone else alive. Am I afraid he wouldn't believe me? I don't know if I believe myself.

I was neither here nor there, in the bathroom and yet not there at all—somewhere in the nowhere space between all spaces. I felt cold tile beneath me, the press of bare flesh and the grate of bone, the steady pulse as I leaked through all the doorways I had opened in myself. Yet all of that was so distant, so *quiet* somehow. In amongst it and everywhere was a sweet lightness, an emptiness I was expanding into, that I longed to be a part of.

The bathroom was there, but it was not the same. All about me was an odorless black smoke that coiled and curled, tentacles of shadow more real than the echoes of that faraway room. Soft black filaments brushed my cheek, explored the seams in my arms, the scores in my thighs. I was alone and yet I was pressed in, surrounded. I heard whispers, a babel of silence, felt the caresses of fingers that were not there, saw faces in the smoke, or the idea of faces. Some I knew. Others . . .

Mum was there. And so was Gran. And cousin Kylie, who died in the car crash when I was little. They pressed around me, shushing, tutting. They spoke all at once and, though nothing they said made sense, I understood all of it. I tried to speak, to tell them I was fine, how happy I was to see them, but no words came out, only ripples in the swirling black.

There were others, too. So many others. The woman from the photo on Christophe's desk, she was there. And old women, old men. Women and men in clothes from other times. Top hats. Parasols. Bonnets, moustaches. This was it, I knew. The last I would ever see. I was between worlds and would soon pass over to the next.

And then the ocean of black seemed to part and the murmurs swelled like a wave drawn back over pebbles, like the chittering of a thousand cockroaches. From within the coiling smoke, someone approached. The others peeled back, turning away from the new arrival as though repelled. Coldness crept into me, and a feeling of dread. I recognized the shape, the movements, but something was wrong, somehow . . . incomplete. It was Sylvie, but she had no face.

Sylvie twirled and danced, those old fluid movements now embodied in smoke. But there was no sad smile, no eyes to flutter. Even here, she was no longer my Sylvie. Less than a ghost in a world of ghosts.

I reached for her with hands of black nothing, while the hands of my body, the meat and bone hands, lay sticky and still on the tiles. There rose a pounding, the throb of blood in my ears.

Then the pounding became a drum beneath me, a furious

hammering and shouts of my name. Then a smash from downstairs and the tinkling of glass. Then silence.

The black smoke enveloped me and there was nothing.

~

I woke to whiteness. Sheer. Stark. Final. My first thought: *So this is how it feels to be dead.*

There was a table and a bowl of grapes. Fluorescent lights above, a bluish-white curtain pulled around. Beside my limp hand, a gray cord ended at a box with a red button. My arms felt tight. I couldn't move my fingers.

Christophe was by my bedside.

"There you are," he said and his eyes sparkled. "I was afraid you weren't coming back."

After the taxi dropped us off from Le Sommet and I had staggered down the street, Christophe had paced around the shop, not knowing what to do with himself. He couldn't relax, couldn't concentrate—too tired to be up, too restless to sleep. He fussed with a pile of books, shuffled estate sale knick-knacks from one tea chest to another. Upstairs in the attic, he sprawled on the leather couch, staring at the bare bulb, the shadows on the ceiling. That, he told me, was when he felt the pull.

He stood, half tumbled down the stairs in his haste. He forgot his nightly routine, didn't lock the shop, left the lights on just as they were. He called an ambulance from the payphone in the street, called them before he even reached my house and found the door locked, the windows dark.

"It was the strangest feeling," he said. "I don't know how, but I just knew something was wrong. I knew you were in there and that I'd find you . . . how I found you. The image was already there in my mind."

I was in the hospital five days, "under observation." I suppose they worried that I'd try to finish the job. Along with the grapes and a pile of dusty Alistair Macleans from the shop, Christophe had brought me some clothes. The nurse took away my belt. When she came with my meal tray—the meat and two gray veg, the white bread and margarine, the juice box and the cup of pink angel fluff—there was only plastic cutlery. The nurse watched while I ate.

"You would have been dead," she delighted in telling me, over and over, "if your father hadn't come home when he did."

I never corrected her and neither did Christophe. Besides, the doctor told me it was my size that saved me. A smaller person would have bled out long before Christophe had kicked down the door.

Sylvie and Dane had driven back to the capital the day after that awful dinner. Christophe told them I'd been called away, a deceased estate in Wagga. He never told Sylvie what happened, and for that I will love him forever.

Epilogos

Sylvie doesn't come round so much anymore. Winter, sometimes; summer, rarely. Last I heard, she was having a baby.

I thought I'd miss her, but I don't. I don't have the time. Things at the shop are busier for me than they've ever been, what with being away half the week, touring the markets and the auctions, going farther and farther afield to plumb the hidden troves. Then back to the attic to sort through the haul, to clean and price and catalog. There's no end to the bedlam, never any shortage of disarray. But it gives me a good feeling to know that, in at least this one corner of the world, I can bring some semblance of order to what would otherwise be chaos.

I haven't trained since that time in the bathroom, not now that the middle fingers of my left hand no longer do what I tell them. The training I do miss. But I've found other ways to redirect that pent-up energy, when my scars start to sing and my whole body crackles with muffled static. Now, I run. Out past the edge of town, away from the highway and the train track that splits the mountain like a sutured wound; out past the lake and the straggle of weatherboards along the ridgeline; out to where the trees thin and the ground drops away and the forested wilderness stretches on forever, fading into a blue haze where it meets the horizon. My feet pound the track, heart aflame in its cage of meat and bone.

I don't think back often to that night, but sometimes there are flashes. I'll be cleaning a ship in a bottle, or pricing silver candelabra, and it's as though I'm back in the smoke-filled bathroom. I'll remember a face, one of the strangers who crowded around me as I lay on the floor, remember them clearer than I ever saw them at the time. Sometimes a man with a moustache. Sometimes a woman with a bonnet. Sometimes faces I don't recognize, but can picture clear as day, limned in coiling black smoke. But then I'll come back, to the attic and the object in my hands, and it'll be just whatever it is right now, here, with none of that other stuff. Just a cigarette box, or a napkin ring, or a soapstone figurine.

I do wonder sometimes about what I saw, there in that halfway place of black smoke and shadow. I wonder about Sylvie, the faceless Sylvie from beyond the bathroom—how could she be both there *and* here? In both places broken. Nowhere her true and complete self.

Sylvie never called them ghosts, but that's what they are. Though I can't see them, sometimes the attic feels close, crowded with all that forgotten history, the weight of all those unremembered lives cooped up within each keepsake and memento. On the bad days it hems me in, the pressure of all that latent meaning; it's invisible to me, yet I still feel it, heavy as a storm that won't break.

On the good days, it's not them I feel but *her*—neither the Sylvie who left to marry Dane, nor the Sylvie of that other place, but *my* Sylvie, the perfect Sylvie of my memory. Those are the days when the attic is dark and moribund and rain pelts the skylight, drumming at the shingles, loudly overflowing the broken gutter. On those days, I forget my chores, leave Christophe tinkering in the shop below. I lay back on the cracked leather couch and let the sadness rise within me like a flood. My flesh tingles and my scars hum, a chorus that sings in ragged harmony of the true ghost of Sylvie and the wound in my heart. It is a melancholy song, and beautiful, of the ghost that lives forever in the wound forever open; the wound that never heals because it is not of the body.

About The Author

J. Ashley-Smith is a British-Australian writer of dark fiction and other materials. His short stories have twice won national competitions and been shortlisted six times for Aurealis Awards, winning both Best Horror ("Old Growth," 2017) and Best Fantasy ("The Further Shore," 2018).

J. lives with his wife and two sons in the suburbs of North Canberra, gathering moth dust, tormented by the desolation of telegraph wires.

Did you enjoy this book?

If so, word-of-mouth recommendations and online reviews are critical to the success of any book, so we hope you'll tell your friends about it and consider leaving a review at your favorite bookseller's or library's website.

Visit us at www.meerkatpress.com for our full catalog.

Meerkat Press
Atlanta

CPSIA information can be obtained
at www.ICGtesting.com
Printed in the USA
FSHW021149090720
71811FS